The
Wedding Dress
Disaster

Written by
Eric Stoffle

Book 6
Created by
Jerry D. Thomas

Pacific Press Publishing Association
Boise, Idaho
Oshawa, Ontario, Canada

Edited by Jerry D. Thomas
Designed by Dennis Ferree
Cover art by Stephanie Britt
Illustrations by Mark Ford

Stoffle, Eric D., 1963-
    The wedding dress disaster / written by Eric Stoffle.
        p.   cm. — (The shoebox kids; 6)
    Summary: On Aunt Angie's wedding day, Maria's
bridesmaid dress turns up missing and Maria is afraid
she will not be able to honor her commitment to be in the
wedding.
    ISBN 0-8163-1355-5 (alk. paper)
    [1. Christian life. 2. Weddings. 3. Family life.
4. Mystery and detective stories.] I. Title. II. Series.
PZ7.S8698We   1997
—dc20   96-18587
                                                    CIP
                                                     AC

97 98 99 00 01 • 5 4 3 2 1

Contents

Other Books in
The Shoebox Kids Series

Hi!

Have you ever been asked to be in a wedding? Maybe someone wanted you to be a junior bridesmaid or an usher. Maybe they wanted you to light the candles or spread flower petals. If you have, you know how crazy the wedding planning and rehearsals can be.

That's what Maria finds out in this Shoebox Kids Mystery! This time, Maria has a real problem. She is excited about being in her aunt's wedding, but everything is going wrong! Should she refuse to be a junior bridesmaid?

This Shoebox story is written by my friend Eric Stoffle. He'll keep you guessing about what will happen to Maria and her special dress. He'll also make you think about what commitment means—about what it means to keep your promises and do what you say you will do.

That's what the Shoebox Kids books are really all about—learning to be a Christian not just at church, but at home, at school, and on the playground. If you're trying to be a friend of Jesus', then the Shoebox Kids books are just what you're looking for!

Can you figure out what happened to Maria's missing dress before she does?

Jerry D. Thomas

The Wrong Dress

"Mom! The phone's ringing. Mom?"

That's funny, Maria thought. *I wonder where Mom is?* Puzzled, she put down her book and hurried to answer the phone. She and Mom were the only two at home because Dad, Chris, and Yoyo were grocery shopping. But now it didn't even look as if Mom was home! *Maybe she's outside*, Maria decided.

"Hello?"

"May I speak to Mr. or Mrs. Vargas?" the man's voice on the other end of the line asked.

"My mom is outside," Maria said. *I hope!* she

7

thought. She had been told never to tell anyone on the phone that she was home alone. "May I ask who's calling?" she asked.

"This is Pastor Hill," the voice said. "Who is this?"

"Hi, Pastor Hill," Maria said. "You know who I am. This is Maria Vargas."

Pastor Hill chuckled. "Hi, Maria."

"May I take a message?" Maria asked. She waited for Pastor Hill to answer. He took a long time before saying anything, as if he were thinking really hard.

"No, thank you. I'll call later," he said. Then he hung up.

Suddenly, Maria saw a brown delivery van driving up outside. Something clicked in her brain, and she hurried to the front window. Not only did the delivery van stop right in front of her house, but Mom was standing in the front yard too. And she was talking to Pastor Hill!

Maria went outside. She stared at her mom and Pastor Hill. Pastor Hill was making a lot of motions with his hands. *How could Pastor Hill be in my front yard talking to my mom?* Maria thought. *I just got through talking to him!*

Pastor Hill smiled. He didn't say anything.

Maria frowned. "Hi, Pastor Hill."

"What's the matter, Maria," Mrs. Vargas asked. "You look puzzled."

Maria wanted to say she had just talked to Pastor Hill on the phone. But then she thought how funny that would sound since Pastor Hill must have been standing right out here in front of their house all the time. If Pastor Hill wasn't the one who called, who was it?

The driver got a package out of his van and walked up to them. Maria had almost forgotten! "It's here! It finally came!"

"What's here?" Mrs. Vargas asked with a knowing smile.

"My dress! The one I get to wear for Aunt Angelina's wedding!" Maria squealed.

The delivery driver handed Mrs. Vargas a box. "Will you please sign this?" he asked, handing over a clipboard.

Maria watched her mom sign her name. Then she waved goodbye to the deliveryman as he walked back to his van. "Can I go try my dress on right now, Mom?"

"Take it inside, and I will be there as soon as I can," Mrs. Vargas said.

Maria went inside and set the box on the

dining-room table. *When Mom comes in, I'm going to tell her about the mysterious phone call*, she decided.

It seemed like hours, but it was really only a few minutes before Mrs. Vargas came back inside. Maria had been concentrating so much on the box with her dress in it that she forgot all about the phone call. She didn't even realize she was impatiently tapping her fingers on the table.

"I'm hurrying as fast as I can, Maria."

"I know, Mom. I'm just so excited. I mean, I've seen the dress in the catalog picture Angelina showed me, but it's just not the same as being able to touch it and put it on. I want to see how pretty it looks on me."

Mrs. Vargas smiled. "I'm sure it will look just beautiful on you, Maria."

Mrs. Vargas slid a small knife along the taped ends of the cardboard box. Soon she pulled up one flap. Then another flap. Maria leaned over the box as far as she could.

As Mrs. Vargas gently lifted the pink dress out of the box, Maria caught her breath. "It's beautiful . . ."

Mrs. Vargas agreed. She held the dress up

and turned it around. Then she got a puzzled look on her face. "I wonder . . . "

Maria waited breathlessly for her mom to say what it was she was wondering.

"Stand here," Mrs. Vargas said.

Maria moved over in front of her mom. Mrs. Vargas held the dress up to Maria's shoulders. She pursed her lips and studied it carefully. "You had better try it on, Maria."

Maria saw the concerned look on Mom's face. "What's wrong?"

"Just go try on the dress, Maria," Mrs. Vargas insisted.

Maria took the dress and went upstairs to her room. She quickly slipped the dress over her head. Then she looked at herself in the mirror. "Oh no!" She exclaimed. "I can't wear this!"

I'm glad Dad, Chris, and Yoyo are grocery shopping, Maria thought as she went downstairs in her bare feet. *I don't want them to see me like this*.

"That doesn't look too short," her mom said when she saw Maria.

"It is too short!" Maria almost shouted. "I can't wear *this* dress to the wedding!"

"Why not? It's very pretty. Especially on you.

11

Did you look in the mirror?"

Maria let out a big sigh. "Of course I looked in the mirror. That's why I don't think I can wear this dress. It's not long enough!"

"It's not *too* short," Mrs. Vargas said. "It's a modest dress."

"But it won't be like all the other bridesmaids' dresses. It won't be long and touch the floor. Can't we fix it?" Maria pleaded. "I don't want to look out of place."

Mrs. Vargas sighed. "If we had the time. But since Ben and Angelina moved their wedding up, we just can't. Their wedding is just two days away."

Maria plopped down on one of the dining-room table chairs and rested her chin on the palms of her hands. "I don't want to be in the wedding."

Mrs. Vargas smiled. "It won't be as bad as you think it will be, Maria."

"Why did Ben and Angie have to make their wedding so soon?" Maria wanted to know. "If they were getting married on the fourth of June like they were supposed to, we would have time to fix the dress."

Mrs. Vargas picked up her dust rag and

started dusting the living room. "Because Ben has been called to be a pastor in Idaho. They need a pastor right away, and both Ben and Angie wanted to be married so they can go together."

While Maria was sitting at the table, she heard a low, familiar noise come from outside. It took her a second to realize the sound was a car pulling into the driveway. "Oh no! Dad and Chris and Yoyo are here!"

She barely made it upstairs before the front door opened.

"Strawberry-Nugget-Blue-Mountain-Ripple ice cream," Maria heard Chris announce as he entered the house. "That's what we're having for dessert."

Maria hurried and slipped out of the dress and put her jeans and shirt back on. She brushed her hair because it looked like she'd just pulled a dress over her head. She didn't want to leave any clues that she had the dress, otherwise she would have to put it on and let Dad see it. Before she went out of her room, she put the dress back in its box and slid it under the bed. But she couldn't get it out of her mind. *What am I going to do?* she thought.

Then she thought about Jenny and DeeDee. They would be at the Shoebox tomorrow. Maybe they would have an idea.

Suddenly she remembered something. *I forgot to tell Mom not to say anything!*

2

"Don't Let Anyone See!"

Maria hurried down the stairs so fast she almost knocked her sister down.

Yoyo held up her hand. "Maria . . ."

Maria didn't wait to listen. She ignored Yoyo and went on down the stairs.

Mom was just finishing dusting when Dad came into the living room, followed by Chris. "Is there anything we can do to help?" Mr. Vargas asked.

"You can vacuum," Mrs. Vargas suggested. "And Chris can take out the garbage. After he cleans his room," she added.

"Aw, Mom," Chris moaned.

Maria wanted to say something quickly to Mom, but if she did, Dad would wonder what the secret was. She tried to look busy and started straightening up the living room, even though she had already straightened it up while Dad and Chris and Yoyo were at the grocery store.

"So, Sunday is the big day," Dad said while unwrapping the cord from the vacuum cleaner to plug it in.

Will Dad think of the dress? Maria wondered. *How much do dads know about weddings? Will he ask if the dress has arrived yet?*

Maria watched her dad push the knob that unlatched the handle on the vacuum cleaner with his foot. She watched him switch the vacuum cleaner on and smiled as the living room filled with noise. Now she could talk to her mom.

But as she opened her mouth to speak, Maria glanced up. *Oh no!* she thought.

Yoyo was standing at the top of the stairs with a brown box in her hands. Maria recognized the box. It was the same box she had just hidden under her bed!

Maria whipped around and ran toward the stairs. But then the vacuum quit. Before she knew what was happening, she lost her balance and started falling. Something jerked at her leg and then let go, and she hit the floor with a *kerrthump*.

She turned her head just in time to see her dad duck as an ugly black thing with brass-colored teeth sailed through the air above his head. It looked like a snake with a long, skinny body.

Dad ducked, then looked at Maria. "Are you OK?" he asked.

Maria felt her face turn red. "Yes, I guess so," she said as she untangled her feet.

"Why were you running?" Dad asked. "You know it's not smart to run in the house."

"I know," Maria said. She hung her head. "I'm sorry."

Dad helped her up. She noticed Yoyo was sitting on the top step looking at her, and Chris was standing behind Yoyo. "Now what was so important?" Dad asked.

Maria closed her eyes. *Now everyone will know about the dress. I wish I could hide.* She took a deep breath and opened her eyes. "The dress I'm supposed to wear at Angelina's wedding came today."

"It did?" Dad looked surprised. "Why didn't you tell us?"

Maria looked at her mom. She looked up at Yoyo and Chris. Then she sighed. "Because I didn't want you to see it. It's . . . it's not long enough. I won't look like the other bridesmaids in their long, flowing dresses. I'll look like I don't even belong at the wedding."

Dad sat down in his chair. He rubbed his chin thoughtfully before looking over at Mom. "There's nothing we can do?" he asked.

"I'm afraid not," Mom answered. "The wedding is on Sunday, and that isn't enough time to send for another dress. There must have been a mix-up when we ordered all the dresses."

Dad looked back at Maria. "What were you going to do? Why keep it a secret?"

Maria shrugged. "I guess I don't know what I was going to do. I thought I would come up with a plan later."

"The dress is very pretty," Maria heard her mom say. "I doubt anyone will notice anything wrong. I was a bridesmaid once when I was in college. It was a very big wedding. We all got the same material and the same pattern so we could make our own dresses. The material was very shiny on one side and dull on the other. Everyone but me knew which was the outside. My mother and I made my dress so the shiny side was on the outside. When I got to the wedding, I saw that I was the only one whose dress was shiny."

"Didn't you feel funny being up front and being different?" Maria asked.

"Yes. I felt very funny. I almost decided not to be a bridesmaid at the wedding. But I went ahead with it anyway. Nobody seemed to care, and it was a beautiful wedding. Many people thought my dress was the most beautiful."

"Probably because you are beautiful," Maria said.

Mrs. Vargas beamed happily. "Why, thank you, Maria."

Maria watched Dad take her mother's hand. "I agree with that," he said. That seemed to make her mother even happier.

But Maria wasn't. *Maybe if I get sick*, she thought, *I won't have to be a junior bridesmaid at the wedding*.

But she knew that wouldn't work either.

More than anything, I want to go to the wedding. I just have to find a way to get around wearing that dress! What am I going to do?

When Maria went to her room, Yoyo was already there, sitting on the bed with the box in her lap. She didn't look up, and Maria didn't say anything to her. She ignored Yoyo as she picked up her clothes and dusted the shelves in her room.

"Why won't you talk to me?" Yoyo finally asked.

Maria stopped. She put her hands on her hips and stared at Yoyo. "I don't want to talk to you because you were nosing around and found that dress. Then you got it out. Now everyone knows that it's not the same as the other bridesmaids' dresses and that I'm going to look silly standing up in front of everyone at the wedding." Maria stopped and took a deep breath.

"But I lost my bouncy ball," Yoyo said.

Maria got a painful look on her face. "What?"

"I lost my bouncy ball. That's how I found your dress. I didn't mean to. I was just looking for my bouncy ball." Tears came to Yoyo's eyes. She looked up at Maria. "I'm sorry."

"Oh, Yoyo," Maria said. She sat down on the

bed and hugged her little sister. "I'm sorry for getting mad at you. I know you didn't mean to spoil anything. The wedding is already spoiled anyway."

"Why is it spoiled?" Yoyo asked.

"Because nothing is going right. I think a wedding should go perfectly."

"Why?"

Maria rolled her eyes toward the ceiling. How could she explain it to Yoyo? "Well, if a wedding goes perfectly, and the bride is beautiful, and the groom is handsome, then the marriage will probably last forever."

Yoyo looked confused. Then she got a big smile. "Does that mean Mommy and Daddy were beautiful and their wedding was perfect?"

Maria shrugged. She hadn't ever actually thought about Mom and Dad having a wedding, too, although Mom had shown her pictures from their wedding. But Yoyo must be right. "Yes, Yoyo. I guess Mom and Dad had a perfect wedding," Maria said.

"Maybe Angie shouldn't get married," Yoyo said. She stuck her legs out straight and studied why one sock was all the way up and the other sock was drooping down around her ankle.

"Why not?" Maria asked.

"You said it was spoiled. Don't you remember?"

"I guess I did say that. What are you doing, Yoyo?"

"Looking at my socks. One is higher than the other."

"Pull the other one up, then," Maria suggested.

"But I don't want them up. I like the sock that's down," Yoyo said.

"Then put the other sock down too," Maria said in exasperation. But then she looked at Yoyo's curls and her little nose that had a little turn up at the end of it and her chubby cheeks. "I meant the wedding is spoiled for me, Yoyo, not Angie," she said more softly.

Yoyo looked up at Maria. "You're so smart, Maria," she said. "I'm glad you're my sister."

Suddenly Maria got an idea. "I know, Yoyo. Why don't we say some vows between us, sort of like people do when they get married. This will be for sisters only. OK?"

"OK. What do we do? What are vows?"

"Slow down, Yoyo." Maria put a finger to her lips. "Shhh." She went over and closed their bedroom door.

Yoyo thought very hard. "Why did you close the door?"

"So Chris won't hear us. He'll just think it's weird, because he's a boy."

3

Secret Vows

Maria sat next to Yoyo on the bed. "OK, Yoyo. Repeat after me. I promise to love my sister."

"I promise to love my sister," Yoyo said eagerly. "Now you have to say it, Maria."

Maria smiled. "OK. I promise to love my sister. Now you repeat, 'through sickness and in health.'"

"Through sickness and health," Yoyo said.

Maria thought hard for a minute, but she thought she remembered most of what ministers had the bride and groom say. "For richer or poorer."

Yoyo frowned. "What's that mean?"

Maria scratched her head. "I guess it means that even if you don't have enough money to buy groceries with, you still love each other. And if you have all the money in the world, you have to spend it together."

"OK. For richer or poor," Yoyo said.

"Till death do us part."

"Till death do us part," Yoyo muttered, not liking the sound of those words. "What else do people say?"

"I don't think they say anything else," Maria said thoughtfully. "I can't remember."

Yoyo frowned. "We should say something else. That last one wasn't very nice."

Maria looked at the serious expression on her sister's face. "What about making up a vow?" she suggested.

Yoyo nodded.

"We could say something like 'we're not just sisters, we're best friends, and we choose to be friends forever.' "

"That's long," Yoyo complained. "But I like it best. Do I have to repeat it?"

Maria smiled. "No. It's all right if you just think it."

Yoyo concentrated. "OK. I did," she said.

"There," Maria said. "Now we've said our vows to each other."

Mom's voice echoed upstairs. "Supper's ready!"

Maria's stomach answered with a growl. "I forgot how hungry I was," she said. "And Mom was making my favorite—split-pea soup and toasted cheese sandwiches! Come on, let's get our hands washed and get downstairs."

Yoyo rushed ahead to the bathroom. When Maria got there, she couldn't help but smile. Yoyo was chasing the soap bar across the counter top with wet little hands.

"Can you help me?" Yoyo asked when she saw Maria. "It keeps running away." Maria stuck one finger on the soap bar and held it until Yoyo could get her little fingers around it.

When Maria finished washing her hands, Yoyo handed her the towel. "Thank you, Yoyo," Maria said. "That was very nice of you."

Yoyo grinned. "I like doing nice things for you because you're my favorite sister," she said proudly.

"She's your only sister," a voice said from the doorway.

Yoyo whipped around. Maria glanced in the mirror and caught Chris laughing at them.

"What are you two talking about?" Chris asked curiously.

Chris hates it when someone has a secret he doesn't know, Maria thought. *Well, too bad for him. He's not part of our secret vow.* She knew her brother well enough to know that he would start teasing them to find out. "Yoyo, follow me," she said as she turned and marched out of the bathroom.

Chris leaned against the doorjamb a moment before standing up straight and chasing after Maria and Yoyo. "Oh, you're going to ignore me, huh? You two are going to try to pretend like I'm not even here?"

The girls gave no answer.

"Well, I'm not going to let you have any dessert," Chris stated, following along behind.

The girls said nothing.

I'm pretty good at this, Maria thought. *Chris can't make me talk if I don't want to. And he can't keep me from having any dessert either.* She smiled.

Chris paused at the top of the stairs as Maria and Yoyo marched down in single file like soldiers. "We don't have to talk to Chris if we don't want to, Yoyo," Maria told Yoyo as if Chris were not even there.

"No," Yoyo agreed. "We stick together."

Finally Chris started downstairs too. "How come you're Maria's best buddy all of a sudden, Yoyo? I thought she was mad at you earlier."

But Yoyo didn't say a word.

Maria sat down in her place at the dinner table, and Yoyo climbed into her chair. Yoyo had just gotten her very own grown-up chair, but she had to sit on her legs.

Chris came in and sat down with a frown on his face.

He must be thinking of new ways to tease us, Maria thought, keeping her smile to herself. She glanced across the table at Chris, but he was ignoring her just like she was ignoring him.

Mr. Vargas asked everyone to hold hands while he asked the blessing. After the blessing was over, he dipped some soup for Yoyo. Maria held out her bowl, and Dad dipped some soup for her too. She reached for the same toasted cheese sandwich that Chris wanted, but she let him have it, and she took another one.

That seemed to confuse Chris even more.

How could Maria be ignoring him and be nice to him at the same time? The look on his face made Maria smile.

"Who is making the wedding cake for Angie and Ben?" Mr. Vargas asked.

"Mrs. Wallace," Mrs Vargas replied.

Surprised, Maria looked up. "Is Jenny going to be at the wedding, since her mom is baking the cake?"

"Why, I don't know, Maria," Mrs. Vargas said.

Maria wasn't sure if she wanted Jenny to be at the wedding or not. *After all, I'm going to look out of place. That is, if I decide to go to the wedding. I may not get to be a junior bridesmaid after all*, she thought.

"Sammy is going to be at the wedding," Chris announced. "He told me today at school."

Maria's spoonful of soup accidentally went down the wrong pipe. "Wh-*ka-ka-what?*" She choked. "Why is Sammy going?"

Chris grinned. "Because his Uncle Loc is going to be taking wedding pictures."

Oh no! Maria thought. *I just can't look funny in the wedding with all the Shoebox Kids there. What am I going to do?*

"What's the matter, Maria?" Mrs. Vargas asked. "You look pale. Are you sick?"

Maria shook her head. She wasn't sick, not really sick anyway. But she wasn't very happy either. *Mom just doesn't understand*, Maria decided. *All I ever wanted to do was wear a long, pretty dress, with lace and ruffles. I wanted to look as beautiful as the bridesmaids, with their long dresses that touch the floor and make them look like princesses. Instead, my dress will only come to my knees.*

Suddenly supper didn't taste so good. *I won't even look like I'm at the right wedding*, Maria thought.

CHAPTER

4

The Perfect Wedding

"Mrs. Shue? Who had the best wedding in the Bible?" Maria asked. Their lesson in the Shoebox was over, and Maria had been wanting to ask her question all morning.

Mrs. Shue's eyebrows went up as she thought. "I believe I like the first marriage the most."

Now everyone's eyebrows went up. No one could think of who Mrs. Shue was talking about.

Willie Teller wasn't afraid to ask. "I can't think. Who had the first wedding?"

Mrs. Shue smiled, but before she could answer, Sammy raised his hand.

"It must have been Jacob," Sammy said without being asked. "He worked hard for seven years to marry Rachel, but instead, his uncle gave him his oldest daughter, Leah, to marry. Then he had to work another seven years to marry Rachel."

"Sammy, you remember that story very well," Mrs. Shue said. "But I'm sorry, I wasn't thinking about Jacob."

"Then who?" Jenny asked.

Suddenly DeeDee grinned. "Was it when Abraham sent his servant to find a wife for Isaac?"

Mrs. Shue slowly shook her head. "No, not Isaac and Rebekah." she said.

Maria sighed. "A lot of people got married in Bible times."

"That's true, Maria," Mrs. Shue replied. "But keep trying. These two people I am thinking about were married by God Himself. Can you imagine how special that must have been?"

Jenny's eyes got big. "Oh! Do you mean Adam and Eve?"

"Right, Jenny," Mrs. Shue said as she reached for her Bible. "Genesis 2:18 says: 'Then the Lord God said, "It is not good for the man to be alone.

I will make a helper who is right for him.' ' "
Mrs. Shue looked at her class. "And in verse 22
it says, 'Then the Lord brought the woman to
the man.' And if we read further, in verse 24, it
says, 'So a man will leave his father and mother
and be united with his wife. And the two people
will become one body' " (ICB).

"I guess that would have to be the most
perfect wedding," Maria agreed. "Since my aunt
is going to be married tomorrow, I was trying to
explain to Yoyo how people stay married. I told
her that if their wedding is perfect, two people
will stay together forever."

Maria didn't see the frown on Jenny's face or
DeeDee shaking her head. Sammy and Willie
seemed confused, but they didn't say anything.

"I think Maria's wrong," DeeDee said. "Don't
they just have to love each other? A perfect
wedding doesn't mean a marriage is going to
last forever."

"I think you have part of the answer, DeeDee,"
Mrs. Shue said. "And Maria, it does help for two
people to get started right when they are married. But there is much more to marriage than
a beautiful wedding."

Jenny raised her hand halfway. When Maria

saw Jenny, she suddenly remembered that Jenny's parents were divorced and that it must be sort of hard for her to talk about weddings and marriages and stuff.

Mrs. Shue smiled. "Yes, Jenny?"

The Shoebox grew quiet as Jenny cleared her throat. "It doesn't always work that way, DeeDee, just like Mrs. Shue said," Jenny said softly. Then she looked at Maria. "Mom said her's and Dad's wedding was beautiful and perfect. She said it was a very happy day. She told me they loved each other very much. But they still got divorced."

Maria stared at the floor. Suddenly, hoping for a perfect wedding seemed silly. *I wanted so much for Angie's wedding to be beautiful, just like the weddings on TV and in books.*

Later, in her room, Maria could hear her mother and sister talking in excited voices about the wedding rehearsal. *I'd be excited, too, if I had a long, pretty dress for the wedding,* Maria thought. *At least, no one has to dress up for the rehearsal. But if I go to the rehearsal and learn what I'm supposed to do, then I'll have to go to the wedding.* She walked slowly down the stairs when it was time to go.

"Why do you look so unhappy?" Mrs. Vargas asked.

"I don't want to go to the rehearsal," Maria replied.

Chris thumped down the stairs behind Maria. "You're still unhappy about that dress? What's the big deal?"

"Leave me alone," Maria mumbled.

Mom patted Chris's arm. "Go on to the car, dear. And leave Maria alone, please."

"At least *I'm* not complaining about going to some wedding rehearsal," Chris said as he headed the rest of the way down the stairs.

"You would if you had to wear a dress that was different from everyone else's," Maria argued.

Chris laughed as he opened the door. "You're right about that. I'd complain if someone wanted me to wear the same dress as anyone else. I'd run away screaming!"

Maria stuck out her tongue at Chris's back, but she could hardly hold back her laugh. *He would look funny in a dress*, she decided.

Dad followed Chris to the door, then turned to Mom and Maria. "Don't be too long," he said. "We don't want to be late for the rehearsal."

"You wait in the car with Chris and Yoyo, dear," Mom said. "Maria and I will be out in a minute."

After Dad had gone, Maria felt like she needed to talk. "Mom, I wish I didn't have to go to the wedding. I wish I didn't have to walk up the aisle in that dress, and I wish I didn't have to stand up front where everyone can look at me and wonder why I'm not wearing a long dress like everyone else. Nothing is going to be the way I dreamed it would be."

Mrs. Vargas hugged Maria. "I'm sorry. I know how much being part of Angie's wedding meant to you. When I was a little girl, I had many of the same dreams about beautiful weddings and princes and princesses that you do."

"You did? Did you dream about having the most beautiful wedding in the world and wearing the most beautiful clothes and stuff like that? Just like in books and things?"

Mrs. Vargas smiled warmly. "Yes, I did. And I did have a beautiful wedding. But there is more to being married than having a beautiful wedding. There is love and trust and commitment."

"What is 'commitment'?" Maria asked.

" 'Commitment' is doing what you say you will do. It means the same thing as making a vow or a promise. When two people say their vows at their wedding, they are making a commitment to each other to do what they have promised. When two people honor their commitment to each other, they are helping their marriage last."

"So a commitment is like keeping a promise?" Maria asked, thinking she understood.

"Yes," Mrs. Vargas said seriously. "Keeping a promise is very much like honoring a commitment. Doing what you say you will do is a very good thing to learn, especially when you are young. The ability to stay committed to something doesn't happen overnight, Maria. It is something we must teach ourselves to do."

Maria's mind was spinning. This sounded like grown-up stuff. And Mom was trying to tell her something important. Maria thought she knew what message Mom was trying to get across too. "Does that also mean that I should be in Angie's wedding even if I don't want to? That since I promised to be a junior bridesmaid, no matter what happens, I should do it?"

"I think you know the answer, Maria."

Maria sighed. "I do, Mom."

CHAPTER

5

A Pain in the Neck

Maria felt sorry for Pastor Hill. Every time he tried to talk, he sneezed. Sometimes he sneezed five sneezes in a row. Maria sat down in a pew until it was her turn to learn her part in the wedding. *If I had a cold like that, I wouldn't have to be in the wedding*, she thought.

Later, while she was practicing walking up the aisle as she was supposed to do at the wedding, she couldn't help but think about the next day when lots and lots of people would be sitting in the pews. *Will they notice my dress?* she wondered. She didn't think she would ever get it out of her mind.

The wedding still wouldn't be anything as she had imagined it would be, but she wasn't going to quit either. Angie and Ben were counting on her to keep her word. Somewhere between talking to her mom about commitment and the end of the rehearsal, she made up her mind. She would stick to her commitment.

Boy, am I tired, Maria thought as the Vargas family piled into the car for the drive home. After fastening her seat belt and making sure Yoyo was fastened in, Maria leaned her head against the window and closed her eyes. She didn't even try to pick out the Big Dipper in the sky or try to find the North Star, as she usually did at night. She could hear her parents talking softly in the front seat.

"Do you think Pastor Hill will be well enough to perform the wedding tomorrow?" her mother asked.

Her dad's voice sounded worried. "I don't know. You could tell he was feeling pretty bad tonight."

That made Maria's eyes pop open for a second. *What will happen if Pastor Hill can't be there?* she wondered. *And I thought my dress was a disaster—Angie might have to put off the whole wedding!*

Thinking about Pastor Hill reminded her of that strange phone call the day her dress arrived. *I forgot to tell Mom or Dad about Pastor Hill being on the phone and in the front yard at the same time. I'd better do that right now.*

But her eyes were closing again. *I'll just rest for a few seconds, then tell them,* she decided.

Two seconds later—it seemed like—Chris was shaking her shoulder. "Hey, Maria! Wake up! We're home."

Sleepily, Maria tried to raise her head, but a sharp pain ran right down one side of her neck. Her head felt as if it didn't want to stay on her shoulders. Her neck hurt too bad to hold it up. She tried holding up her head with her hands, but she quickly discovered she couldn't open her door at the same time.

I must have a kink in my neck from sleeping like that. What am I going to do? Maria thought. *Mom and Dad were already out and unlocking the front door. Yoyo must have slid out on Chris's side, so she can't help.*

Suddenly, Chris's face was smashed up against the outside of her window. "WWHHAATT

AARREEYYOOUU DOOIINNGG?" He mouthed the words and steamed up the window.

Maria groaned. *Oh, great! Chris will just laugh at me because my neck won't work right. I'm just not having a very good week!* Trying to smile as pleasantly as possible, she turned her head as far as she could toward the window.

Chris's grin was stuck to her window. "Please open the door," she asked.

To her surprise, Chris didn't laugh or make stupid faces or yell loud enough to the whole neighborhood that his sister had a kink in her neck. Instead, he opened the door with a wide, sweeping bow. "There you are," he said nicely.

Too nicely, Maria thought. Carefully, she moved her legs out of the car and stood up. "Thank you, Chris."

"No problem, sis," Chris replied with a smile.

"I thought you would do something dumb," Maria said.

Chris acted shocked. "Who, me?"

"Yes, you! You *are* my brother. I think I know you well enough by now." Maria thought it would be a good idea to keep an eye on Chris as she started toward the house, but her head could only be pointed in one direction.

Slamm! She heard the car door close behind her. Then she heard another sound—a very loud sound.

"Yeeeeow!" Chris screamed as if he had slammed something in the car door—maybe his whole head.

With the kink in her neck, Maria didn't think her head would even turn. But she just knew Chris had hurt himself badly. Her head was turning before she could stop it. And it hurt— almost as much as it hurt to see Chris standing there with a grin on his face.

"That was mean!" she yelled as she rubbed her neck. "It was a cruel joke to play! I really thought you were hurt!"

Raising his hands, Chris wiggled all his fingers. "But I'm not. Aren't you glad?"

Maria sighed and turned around. Sometimes she thought she had one brother too many.

Chris trotted up beside her as they entered the house. "How's your neck?" he asked.

"It still hurts, thanks to you," Maria grumbled.

Chris's smile disappeared. "I'm sorry. I guess that wasn't a very nice thing to do. Do you want me to rub your neck for you? Or I can go find the heating pad. Mom likes to use that when she's got a sore neck."

Maria frowned. "How can brothers be so mean one minute and nice the next?"

Chris only shrugged and walked off to find their mom. "It was a pretty mean joke, wasn't it?" he called back.

"It sure was," Maria answered. "But it proves that what I've been telling everyone is true—you really are a pain in the neck." Chris laughed and Maria headed up to her room. She had to take two looks at her clock to be sure of the time, and she still couldn't believe it was so late. She quickly changed into her pajamas and crawled under the covers.

Yoyo already had her pajamas on, but before climbing into bed, she stopped by Maria's room. "Goodnight, Maria."

Maria smiled. "Goodnight, Yoyo."

"Are you going to be in the wedding?" Yoyo asked.

Maria started to nod, but stopped quickly. "Ow! I guess so," she answered as she rubbed her neck again.

"Do you have to, even if you don't want to?" Yoyo wanted to know.

"I said I would be in it for Aunt Angie, so I will. It won't be so bad. I'll just be different." Maria tried to explain. "It would be selfish for me not to be in the wedding just because I don't like the dress I'm supposed to wear."

Yoyo didn't move. She was thinking very hard. Maria yawned and closed her eyes.

"I could help," Yoyo offered. But Maria didn't hear. She was already asleep.

Maria didn't hear Mom and Dad come in and kiss her goodnight. She didn't hear Chris when he left the heating pad on the chair by her dresser.

6

"It's Missing!"

Bright shafts of light streamed through Maria's bedroom window. When the alarm clock buzzer buzzed for the tenth time, a hand shot out from underneath the pillow and covers and shut it off.

"You better get up, Maria! We have to leave in an hour for the church!" Mr. Vargas's rich baritone voice called from downstairs. *Why does Dad always have to sound so happy in the morning?* Maria wondered as she started to drag herself out of bed.

Suddenly, Maria's eyes flashed open. *Today*

51

is Aunt Angie's wedding day! She must be really happy! And I should be happy for her too. Somehow, this was the first time Maria thought about being happy for Angie instead of feeling sorry for herself. *I really have been selfish*, she decided.

All at once, she was eager to go to the wedding. She flung the covers off and stood up. "Hey," she said out loud, "my neck doesn't hurt at all." Just to test it out, she tossed her black hair behind her shoulders with a flick of her head.

After showering quickly, she dressed in a pair of nice jeans and a shirt. Before leaving her room to go downstairs to eat breakfast, she took the dress out of her closet and laid it on the bed.

As usual, Mr. Vargas was pacing back and forth waiting for everyone to get in the car so they could leave. He glanced at his watch and paced harder. "Maria! Yoyo! Chris!" he called upstairs.

"Coming," Chris said.

"I'm coming, too," Yoyo announced as she lugged her doll, Liberty, and a pink suitcase full of doll clothes downstairs.

Chris was right behind her. He was wearing his blue suit. "What are you going to do with Liberty and all those clothes, Yoyo?"

"Going to dress her up for the wedding," Yoyo said.

Maria was carrying her dress. She went outside and got in the car with Yoyo and Chris. Mom and Dad came out a few minutes later, and soon they were on their way to Angie's wedding.

Mrs. Vargas started going through her checklist. "Everyone have their seat belts fastened?"

"Yes," Chris, Yoyo, and Maria said in unison.

"Yoyo, did you bring your blue barrettes for me to put in your hair?"

"Uh-huh."

Mrs. Vargas turned her head to see Chris. "You certainly look nice, Chris."

Maria felt sort of funny being the only one in the family who wasn't dressed up already. But Mom had said it would be a good idea to wait and get dressed at the church. That way nothing disastrous would happen to the dress before the wedding.

Maria gazed out the window. Springtime was her favorite time of the year. It was warm outside. The trees and grass and flowers smelled pretty. Suddenly she was incredibly happy. *This is going to be the best wedding*, she decided. *Angie and Ben are going to have a beautiful wedding, and I'm going to be part of it!*

When they drove into the church parking lot and got out, Mrs. Vargas noticed Maria's happy attitude. "You seem awfully happy all of a sudden, Maria," she said.

Maria laughed. "I am. This is going to be the best wedding. I'm happy for Angie."

Maria locked her arm in her mom's, and they walked into the church together. Maria even felt like skipping. She felt so happy all of a sudden that she was sure *nothing* could ruin the day. Absolutely nothing!

Several people were already unloading stuff in the multipurpose room for the reception that would start after the wedding. Mrs. Swartz, one of the deaconesses, came over and asked Mrs. Vargas if she could help cover tables and arrange centerpieces. "Hello, Maria," she said after a moment.

"Hi, Mrs. Swartz."

When Mrs. Swartz saw the dress, she drew in a deep breath and seemed to be genuinely admiring it. "Why, that is beautiful, Maria! I'm sure you look very pretty in it!"

Maria blushed. She sort of wished she could run and put it on right away.

"She is absolutely beautiful in it," Mrs. Vargas agreed, winking at Maria.

Maria knew what the wink meant. It meant that Mom had been right all along and that most of the time, moms *were* right and that their children should try to remember it. Maria smiled back. "Can I go put it on right now?" Maria asked after Mrs. Swartz had left.

"Let's wait for a while," Mrs. Vargas suggested. "I need to help with the tables first. "Why don't you lay the dress on this table while I go find a hanger to hang it on."

Maria noticed that some mother had left a diaper bag on the table, too, and she wondered whom it belonged to. When she looked around, all she could see was a strange man holding a small baby. *The diaper bag must belong to him*, Maria thought.

Just then, Jenny opened a door, and Mrs. Wallace came in holding a wide box. She gently carried it over to another table and set it down. Maria thought she could see beads of perspiration on Mrs. Wallace's forehead.

"Hi, Jenny," Maria called.

Jenny saw Maria and waved. Mrs. Wallace went out and brought in one more big box and set it beside the first box.

"Hi, Maria," Jenny said when her mother came back in and she could close the door. "You must be really excited."

Maria smiled. "I'm a little nervous. I probably won't even be able to walk up the aisle by the time the wedding starts."

"Jenny, will you help me set up the wedding cake?" Mrs. Wallace asked. She had already taken the biggest cake out of its box and set it on the table. Jenny very carefully lifted the second biggest cake to her mother. Maria didn't think she had ever seen a cake so beautiful. It was round and had three layers, and each layer was held up by four white columns. It made her think of pictures she had seen of buildings that had white marble columns.

Mrs. Wallace took the last layer and carefully set it on top. Maria giggled when Mrs. Wallace finally took her hands away from the cake, because everyone seemed to have been holding their breath, even Maria. But Mrs. Wallace took the biggest breath when it was finished. She sighed and let her shoulders drop.

"Whew," she said. "I'm glad that's finished."

"It's the most beautiful cake I've ever seen, Mrs. Wallace," Maria exclaimed. "How do you make all those flowers and leaves?" Maria stepped a little closer to the cake but not too close. She didn't want something to accidentally happen to it.

"Thank you, Maria. I must say, it takes a lot of time and patience to make all those flowers." Mrs. Wallace started to explain how to make flowers out of frosting. "First, you put a piece of wax paper on a little plastic stick with a platform on it. Then take a tube of frosting with a wide, thin tip on it. Twirl the stick—"

"Oh no!" Maria's hand flew up to her mouth as she looked over Mrs. Wallace's shoulder. "Look!"

7

Wedding Dress Disaster

Everyone stared in the direction Maria was pointing. Maria had been looking at Mrs. Wallace, but suddenly she noticed that she could also see the table where she had left her dress. And she could see that the dress wasn't there! "My dress!" Maria cried.

Mrs. Wallace had whirled around, expecting to see her cake horribly mangled or falling over or some child grabbing a chunk of it and trying to shove it into his mouth. When she saw that the cake was OK, she dropped onto a chair and started to fan herself. She didn't hear anything about the dress.

"Sorry, Mrs. Wallace," Maria apologized as she grabbed Jenny by the sleeve and dragged her over to the table. "My dress was right here. But now it's gone."

"Maybe your mom has got it," Jenny suggested.

Maria smiled and relaxed. "Yeah, Mom's probably got it." After a quick glance around the multipurpose room, she located her mom and hurried over. "Did you find a hanger for my dress and hang it up?"

"No, I haven't looked for a hanger yet," Mrs. Vargas said. "I'm going to be decorating these tables for a while too. Could you go ask for a hanger?"

"But, Mom, I can't—"

"Sure you can, Maria," her mom said without looking at her. She was trying to fix a centerpiece so the flowers wouldn't all droop to one side.

Maria wanted to shout, but she remembered what had happened to Jenny's mother a few minutes earlier, and she didn't want to scare anyone else. *Jenny and I will just hunt for the dress ourselves*, Maria thought.

She turned to Jenny. "Mom thinks my dress

is where I left it. But I left it right over there on the table, and it's not there now. Someone must have stolen it."

Jenny frowned. "Maybe someone just moved it out of the way so it wouldn't get dirty. Maybe someone hung it up."

Maria realized Jenny made sense, especially since they *were* in a church, and people don't usually steal when they're in a church. But somebody must have taken it. "Let's go over and investigate," she said, leading Jenny back to the table. "It was lying right here, and some guy's diaper bag was right beside it."

Jenny giggled. "Some guy's diaper bag? Don't you mean some baby's diaper bag? At least, the stuff inside must belong to a baby."

"Well, some guy was holding a baby," Maria replied. "It probably belonged to them. But I don't see him anywhere. And the diaper bag is gone too."

Jenny finally realized what Maria was saying. "Maybe the mysterious man stole the dress! Do you think he could have put it in the diaper bag so no one would see him take off with it?" Jenny's eyes had grown as round and big as saucers.

They both stood and stared for a moment, trying to decide what to do next. "We can't just find him and steal the bag back," Maria said. "We'll have to find my dad or Pastor Hill. Come on, let's go."

They had only gone three steps when Jenny grabbed Maria's arm. "What if it was Chris?" she asked. "I saw him over here when I was holding the door for my mom. He could have taken it as a joke."

Maria didn't know what to say exactly. Chris probably *had* taken the dress. It would be just like him—just as bad as the joke he played last night. "I guess you're right. Let's go find him."

Maria and Jenny checked the lobby and the hallways, but Chris wasn't there. Next, they walked out to the gym to see if he was shooting baskets. But there were only two younger kids playing in the gym.

"He's probably outside," Jenny said.

Maria opened a door and went outside. The parking lot was filling up with cars, and Maria suddenly thought of something. "I don't have much time before I have to change. We have to find my dress!"

Maria and Jenny walked around the church

until they were back at the front door, but Chris seemed to have disappeared.

"Isn't that Sammy's uncle's car over there?" Jenny pointed out.

Maria smiled. "Yeah. Chris said Loc was taking the wedding pictures. Maybe Chris is with Sammy."

"*Maybe?* I'm sure he is if Sammy's here. They probably planned taking the dress together, and now they're hiding out somewhere so we can't find them. Or worse, they're probably watching us hunt for them this very minute. Sometimes boys are such brats!"

Maria looked at Jenny and laughed. "I was just thinking the same thing last night when Chris tricked me into turning my head even though I had a stiff neck."

Yoyo was standing in the lobby with her pink suitcase and Liberty when Maria and Jenny went back inside.

"Hi, Yoyo," Jenny said.

"Hi, Yoyo," Maria said.

Jenny knelt down in front of Yoyo. She looked at Yoyo's doll. "She is a very pretty doll. What's her name?"

"Liberty," Yoyo answered.

"Do you have clothes for Liberty in the suitcase? Can I look at them?"

"No. I just changed her for the wedding. Liberty doesn't want to be changed again." Yoyo said.

"But I just wanted to look at her clothes. Maybe I have some doll clothes at home that will fit Liberty. If they're the same size, I could give them to you," Jenny said.

Yoyo thought the offer over. She held Liberty close to her ear so she could hear what her doll had to say. "I'm sorry, Jenny," Yoyo said in as big a voice as she could, "but Liberty says she doesn't want to wear old clothes."

"But they wouldn't be old clothes to her," Jenny tried to explain.

Yoyo shrugged and picked up her little pink suitcase. "We have to go sit down now."

Maria was getting impatient. "Come on, Jenny. If we don't find my dress, it's going to be a disaster. The wedding plans will be all upset, and I won't be able to be a junior bridesmaid after all." They walked passed Yoyo and went into the sanctuary.

Yoyo stopped walking. "I thought you didn't want to wear the dress, Maria," she said. But Maria and Jenny had already gone.

8

The Mysterious Stranger

Chris doesn't look very guilty, Maria thought as she and Jenny entered the sanctuary where some more people were getting ready for the wedding. Chris was standing beside Sammy as they watched Sammy's Uncle Loc set up his camera equipment. Elder Jansen and his wife were making sure all the candles and flowers were in the right position up front.

When Mrs. Jansen saw Maria, she waved and came down the aisle. "Hi, Maria. I'm glad you stopped in before the wedding. We had to change where you will be standing during the ceremony, so let me show you the piece of tape that you need to stand on."

Maria followed as Mrs. Jansen talked. "Now, when you walk up, you will want to make a sharper turn when you pass the first pew. Right about here. We had to move everyone back about ten inches."

Maria studied her position. She stepped on the tape and made sure she knew exactly which way to stand. "Is this right!"

Mrs. Jansen nodded and smiled. "Yes. You shouldn't have any problem."

I will if I can't find my dress, Maria thought. "Is that all?" she asked, looking up. She suddenly caught her breath and pointed. "Who's that?" she almost shouted.

Mrs. Jansen looked toward the doors. "Who is who?" she asked Maria. "I don't see anyone."

"Didn't *you* see him, Jenny?"

Jenny looked toward the doors too. "I wasn't looking, Maria."

"It was the same guy I told you about earlier. The guy with the baby and the diaper bag. Can I go now, Mrs. Jansen?" Maria asked.

"Are you sure you'll remember what you are supposed to do?"

Maria nodded and quickly walked over to Chris and Sammy. Jenny was right behind her. "I have to get dressed right away for the wedding, Chris. So I need to get my dress back."

Chris got a puzzled look on his face. "So? I don't know where your dress is."

"You took it to play a trick on me," Maria insisted. "But it's not funny."

Chris shrugged. "But I've been with Sammy since I got here. You can even ask Sammy."

"Chris has been with me, all right," Sammy said. "And I've been with my uncle."

Maria crossed her arms and made an "umph" sound. "How come I don't believe you, Chris?" She thought back to the trick with the car door last night and all the other things he did to tease her. "You're always doing something to try and be funny."

Chris shrugged again. "But I didn't take your dress. I haven't even seen it since you brought it in from the car. Are you sure it's missing?"

"We've looked everywhere," Jenny said. "No one in the multipurpose room remembers seeing it."

Chris narrowed his eyes as if he were thinking hard. "It sounds like a mystery to me."

Maria threw up her hands. "It *is* a mystery. Unfortunately, I don't have all day to solve it!" Whipping around, she started to walk out. *Now what will I do?* she wondered. But just as quickly as she thought it, she seemed to have an answer. *I know, I'll pray.* She stopped just before leaving the sanctuary and bowed her head. "Dear Jesus, I know I was selfish, and I didn't want to wear the dress in the first place, but I know that I should also do what I promised. Please help me find the dress soon enough that I can be in the wedding. Amen."

Maria didn't realize she was being followed until she stopped in the lobby. "What are you guys doing?" she asked Chris and Sammy.

"We thought we would help you find your dress," Chris said. "It made me feel bad when you didn't believe me. I really am sorry for playing that trick on you last night with the car door too."

Maria took a deep breath. "Thanks—we have a better chance of finding it now that there are four of us searching. Come on, let's go."

"There you are, Maria!" A woman's voice said.

Maria's heart sank. She looked at the long,

beautiful pink dress, then she looked at the person wearing it. Molly was one of the bridesmaids. "Hi, Molly. It's not time to start yet, is it?"

"Pretty soon. Angie wanted to see you before the wedding started."

Maria was getting really worried. She didn't know where the dress was, and now Angie wanted to see her. *What if Angie asks if I'm ready?* Maria thought. *I can't tell her the dress is lost.*

Maria couldn't believe how beautiful her aunt looked when she went into the room where Angie was getting ready for the wedding. There seemed to be so much happiness in the room. She quietly stood out of the way until Angie saw her.

"Oh, Maria. I'm glad I got to see you before the ceremony started," Angie said when she saw her.

"You look beautiful, Angie," Maria said as she admired Angie's white gown.

"Thank you, Maria. I hoped I would get to see you in your dress too."

Maria cleared her throat. How could she tell Angie that she didn't know where her dress was?

But Angie began talking again. "I'm sorry your dress is short and not long like it was supposed to be. I must have placed the order wrong. I know how much you were looking forward to wearing a long dress."

Maria smiled. "My dress is beautiful too."

Angie glanced at her watch. "The wedding will be starting pretty soon. Did you see many people out there, Maria? Did you see Ben? Does he look handsome?"

I've got to tell Angie I can't find my dress! Maria suddenly realized she was tapping her foot like she always did when she got nervous. "Lots of people are coming," she answered. "I saw Ben once. He looked nervous. He's handsome. I don't know where my dress is." Maria blurted it all out so fast she wasn't exactly sure what she said.

"You don't know where your dress is?" Angie asked.

"I'm sorry. Somebody must have taken it. I set it down on a table in the multipurpose room, and then it just disappeared."

Angie didn't get mad or upset or anything. She simply knelt down in front of Maria and asked if she had a plan.

"Well," Maria started. "Chris and his friend, Sammy, and my friend Jenny are trying to find it right now. But it's almost too late."

"I think I can hold up the wedding a little while if it is necessary," Angie suggested with a grin. "After all, I'm the bride—it's my wedding."

"But won't everyone get upset?" Maria asked.

Angie looked straight into Maria's eyes. "I don't think anyone will be as upset as I would be if you weren't able to take part in my wedding. The first time I saw you—when you were just a baby—I wanted you to have a part in my wedding. I don't think a few more minutes will make much difference."

"Thank you, Angie." Maria gave her a huge hug. "I love you."

Maria hurried out and found Chris and Sammy and Jenny. "Angie said she'll wait until we find my dress. But we have to hurry!"

Sammy cleared his throat. "Umm, was the man with the baby wearing a gray suit?"

"Yeah, I think so," Maria said. "Why? Do you know where he is?"

"Is that him?"

9

A Trap to Catch a Thief

"That's him!" Maria whispered excitedly. The mysterious man slipped into the pastor's study. Maria turned to her friends. "Let's go see what he's doing."

Maria crept silently up to the pastor's study door and put her finger to her lips to warn Chris, Sammy, and Jenny not to make any noise.

Sammy and Jenny sneaked to the other side of the door and got as close as they dared without being seen. All of them heard the strange man pick up the phone and push the buttons to call someone.

"Hi. It's me," he said. Don't worry, I've done this before. No one will notice anything . . ."

Maria clamped a hand over her mouth. Her eyes felt like they would pop out.

The man's voice continued. "It will work out perfectly. I've gone over the plan several times. I put it in the diaper bag so I wouldn't forget it."

Maria's heart was pounding so hard she felt sure everyone could hear it. Creeping very softly, they sneaked back down the hall.

"Did you hear him?" Maria asked.

Jenny looked really worried. "Maybe we should call the police," she suggested.

Just then Yoyo walked up with her pink suitcase. She tugged on Maria's shirt. "What are you doing?" she asked.

"Shhh . . . We're trying to catch a thief," Maria said.

Yoyo looked worried. "How do you catch a thief?"

Without actually thinking about it, Maria said, "Well, you have to learn to think like a thief thinks. Then you have to catch him with the stuff he stole."

Yoyo frowned. "I don't know how a thief thinks. I only wanted to help."

"You're too young to catch a thief, Yoyo," Chris stated.

"No one wants to listen to me," Yoyo murmured.

"Oh no! Here he comes!" Jenny whispered. "Try to act normal."

The strange man came out of the pastor's study with the diaper bag hanging on his shoulder. He smiled at the Shoebox Kids as he walked by. Maria tried to fake a smile, but she discovered it was hard to smile when she was scared.

"I'm sure my dress is in that diaper bag," Maria insisted when the man had gone.

Jenny agreed. "The diaper bag was sitting right beside Maria's dress, and that man was not too far away. It must have been him!"

Yoyo started tugging on Maria's shirt again. "But I thought you didn't want to wear the dress."

"I want to now," Maria said. She followed the mysterious man to see where he was going. Chris, Sammy, and Jenny were following right behind her. Yoyo picked up her pink suitcase and followed too.

"Why do you suppose he has a diaper bag but he doesn't have a baby?" Chris asked.

"He was holding a baby earlier," Maria replied. "Wait! Look! He's heading toward the baby room! He doesn't even have a baby!"

"Maria!" Mrs. Vargas's voice said, startling Maria. "Why aren't you dressed for the wedding? I've been looking all over for you."

Maria stuttered. "B-b-but . . ." She looked at her friends and Chris for help, but no one seemed to know what to say. Yoyo put her suitcase down and plopped down on top of it. She rested her chin in the palm of her hand and watched.

"Oh, well," Mrs. Vargas said in a frazzled tone of voice, "the bride seems to be having problems getting ready on time too. Have you seen the pastor? I need to tell him Angie isn't ready yet."

They all shook their heads. None of them had seen Pastor Hill. But Maria wasn't thinking about Pastor Hill. She let out a big sigh of relief. Angie was holding up the wedding, just for her. *Angie is so cool*, she thought.

As soon as Mrs. Vargas left, Maria spoke up. "I'm out of time! We have to make a plan for catching this dress thief. How are we . . . wait a minute! I've got a great idea!" She snapped her fingers. "This is going to work," she added.

Chris made a face. "I've got an idea too. Let's move a chair in front of the nursery and not let him out until he hands over the dress."

"That won't work," Sammy answered. "Maria needs the dress now, not when that guy gives up. Besides, some adult will open the door for him. We have to find someone to tell—someone who will help us catch him."

"We need Pastor Hill," Jenny decided. "Where is he?"

"Wait a minute, everyone," Maria said. "If nobody likes my plan, we can choose another one. I think it will work."

She huddled everyone together and explained. Chris and Sammy looked at each other with wide grins, then looked at her. "That is a good plan," Chris said. "Let's do it."

Maria knelt down in front of Yoyo, who still looked sad. "Yoyo, do you want to help us?"

Yoyo shrugged. "What do you want me to do?"

"Can we use Liberty to help catch the thief?"

"I guess so," Yoyo said. She handed Liberty to Maria.

Sammy looked doubtful. "How are we going

to make him think Yoyo's doll needs to be changed?"

Chris smiled. "Like this. Let me see Liberty, Maria." Chris took Yoyo's doll over to the drinking fountain. In a few seconds, Liberty had wet pants. "Here you go, Yoyo. You have to hold Liberty when we go into the baby room."

Yoyo didn't look too happy.

"What's the matter, Yoyo?" Maria asked.

"I don't feel good. I wanted to be your best sister," Yoyo tried to explain.

Maria was confused, but she didn't have time to figure out what was troubling Yoyo.

"Come on, before he leaves." Chris interrupted. He motioned everyone toward the baby room.

Maria held Yoyo's hand. "Can we talk about this later, Yoyo?"

"I guess so."

Maria wondered if Chris and Sammy and Jenny were as nervous as she was. The mysterious man was sitting beside a woman with brown hair and a pretty smile, who was holding a tiny baby. Maria recognized the baby as the same one the man had been holding earlier in the multipurpose room. *That must mean she is the baby's mother*, Maria thought. She smiled when the man and woman turned to see who was coming into the baby room. *They don't really look like thieves*, Maria thought suddenly.

"Hi," Maria said.

"Hi," the mysterious man said back.

Maria got bumped from behind.

"Let us in!" Chris whispered.

Maria scooted forward so everyone could come inside. "Yoyo's doll . . . uh . . . has a wet diaper. We were wondering if you . . . uh . . . had a diaper we could use. Yoyo is my sister."

The woman, who Maria was sure had the nicest smile she had ever seen, seemed to understand. "Oh, Dan, would you get one of Tracy's diapers out of the diaper bag and give it to Yoyo?"

"Sure," the mysterious man said. He got up and picked up the diaper bag from the floor.

What will he do? Maria wondered. *If he opens the diaper bag, my dress will be there. He'll be guilty of taking my dress.* But Dan didn't seem to care if he were caught or not. He set the diaper bag on a chair and with a quick movement, unzipped the bag.

Maria felt Yoyo give her hand a big squeeze.
She felt herself take a deep breath.
But the dress wasn't there!

10

"Call the Police-Quick!"

Chris stared at the open diaper bag. Suddenly, he was very serious. "He didn't take your dress, Maria. He took Yoyo's doll clothes!"

Maria couldn't believe Chris. Even *she* knew what had happened now. "Some detective you are, Chris," she said, rolling her eyes.

"But what did I say?" Chris asked innocently. "Can't you see what's in the bag? He's got all Yoyo's doll clothes."

"I'm sorry, but I have no idea how Yoyo's doll clothes found their way into our diaper bag," Dan said. "By the way, my name is Pastor Hill."

Chris's eyes got even bigger. "Now he's trying to pretend he's Pastor Hill! We've got to call the police!"

Sammy shook his head sadly and put his hand on Chris's shoulder to keep him from running to a phone. Maria could tell that Sammy wanted to laugh. It appeared as though everyone but Chris knew what had happened. But if Chris didn't figure it out soon, she was afraid he really would call the police.

"Maria? Are you in there? Is Pastor Hill in there?" Mrs. Vargas asked from the doorway.

Jenny moved from in front of the door, and she nudged Sammy and Chris out of the way, too, so Mrs. Vargas could come in.

Mrs. Vargas looked puzzled. "I'm glad I found you, Pastor Hill." Suddenly she stopped talking when she thought to wonder why everyone was packed in the baby room. "What are you doing in here, Maria?"

"I was looking for my dress."

"But in here?" Mrs. Vargas asked.

Maria pointed. "We thought he took my dress and hid it in the diaper bag." Maria knew what she said didn't sound very good. Moms always wanted explanations to sound reasonable.

"He said he was Pastor Hill, Mom," Chris announced.

Maria rolled her eyes again. Jenny finally snickered. And Sammy looked like he was just about ready to give up.

Mrs. Vargas smiled and sat down. "Maybe I deserve an explanation about what is going on," she said. "Maria?"

First of all, Maria knelt down. "May I have your doll suitcase, Yoyo?" she asked.

Yoyo silently gave Maria her pink suitcase. Maria laid it on the floor and opened it.

"B-b-b-but . . ." Chris stammered, but he couldn't finish his sentence.

Maria held up her pink dress and gave it to her mom. Then she looked at Yoyo. "Why did you take the dress, Yoyo?"

Yoyo wanted to cry, but she held it in. "I didn't want you to have to wear the dress if you didn't want to." She sniffled and rubbed her eyes.

"So you took the dress and hid it so I wouldn't have to be in the wedding?"

Yoyo nodded. "I'm sorry. I just wanted to be your best sister."

Maria hugged Yoyo. "You are my best sister, Yoyo. Now we should apologize for causing all this trouble."

Maria stood up. "I'm sorry for thinking you took my dress, Pastor Hill," Maria said. Pastor Hill smiled. Mrs. Hill smiled. And Maria thought their little baby was smiling too.

Yoyo wiped her eyes and looked up at Pastor Hill. "I'm sorry," she said.

Finally Maria turned to Chris. "Have you figured it out yet?" She could tell her brother was still puzzled.

"I guess so. Yoyo didn't think you would have to be in the wedding if you couldn't find your dress, so she took her doll clothes out of her little suitcase to make room for your dress. But she didn't have any place to put the doll clothes, so she stuffed them in the diaper bag," Chris said.

"Right," Maria said. "What don't you understand? You still look confused."

Chris sighed in exasperation. "Why is everyone calling *him* Pastor Hill?"

"Oh!" Maria laughed. "So you can't *always* solve a mystery, huh?"

"So?"

Maria couldn't stop laughing. "This Pastor Hill is our Pastor Hill's brother. Our Pastor Hill is sick and can't talk, so he asked his brother to take his place. That's what he was talking about on the phone when we overheard him. And he is the same man who called that day my dress came. Now it doesn't seem so strange that he said he was Pastor Hill when Pastor Hill was outside talking to Mom at the same time."

Suddenly, Mrs. Vargas jumped up. "Oh, my! We better get you dressed, Maria!"

"You had the most beautiful wedding in the world, Angie!" Maria said at the reception. "You were so beautiful!"

"It all did turn out perfect, didn't it?" Angie smiled. "And I'm especially glad you found your dress!"

Maria shook Uncle Ben's hand. But before she went to get her juice and a piece of cake, she whispered in Angie's ear. "Thank you for asking me to be in your wedding." Angie just smiled.

"Maria, over here," Jenny called from a table in the corner.

Balancing her cake and trying not to spill her juice, Maria made her way to the table. "It was just perfect," Jenny said. "Everything was beautiful—and so were you, Maria."

Chris and Sammy rolled their eyes, but Maria

could tell by their smiles that they thought it was a nice wedding too. She blushed a little, then changed the subject so everyone would quit looking at her.

"I'm sure glad we didn't call the police to arrest this Pastor Hill," she said to Jenny. "He's really nice. And that baby Tracy is so cute! Oh, Chris, Pastor Hill was looking for you."

Chris chewed one edge of his lip. "What did he want? Was he mad at me for calling him a thief?"

Maria shrugged. "I don't know. Maybe he's just being friendly."

Chris looked around nervously, then stood up. "I'm through eating. Come on, Sammy. Let's go!"

"Goh wheah?" Sammy asked through a mouthful a cake.

"Just anywhere," Chris answered as he dragged his friend out of the room.

"Do you think Pastor Hill is really mad?" Jenny whispered.

Maria laughed. "No! I think he's going to ask Chris to help him take care of our Pastor Hill's yard this week. I was just playing a joke on Chris."

They both stared as Chris and Sammy peeked around one edge of the doorway to the hall. As the boys ducked down to sneak away, Jenny giggled. "Poor Chris! I hope he figures it out before too long. Maria, your aunt had a beautiful wedding—once the wedding part started. Before that, I thought it was going to be a disaster."

Maria nodded. "It almost was. First, I didn't like the dress, then I couldn't find the dress, then Chris wanted to arrest the pastor! I never thought Yoyo would do something like that just to help me."

"I'm just glad it's all over," Jenny said. "Who knows what will happen next around here!"

"You never know," Maria agreed with a shake of her head. "You never know."